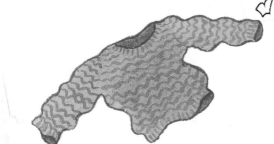

For Peter and Laura
—A.S.C.

I Can Read Book® is a trademark of HarperCollins Publishers.

Biscuit and the Lost Teddy Bear   Text copyright © 2011 by Alyssa Satin Capucilli   Illustrations copyright © 2011 by Pat Schories
All rights reserved. Manufactured in China. No part of this book may be used or reproduced in any manner whatsoever
without written permission except in the case of brief quotations embodied in critical articles and reviews. For information
address HarperCollins Children's Books, a division of HarperCollins Publishers, 10 East 53rd Street, New York, NY 10022.
www.icanread.com

Library of Congress Cataloging-in-Publication Data is available.
ISBN 978-0-06-117751-4 (trade bdg.) — ISBN 978-0-06-117753-8 (pbk.)

13 14 15   SCP   10 9 8 7 6 5 4   ❖   First Edition

Biscuit and the Lost Teddy Bear

story by ALYSSA SATIN CAPUCILLI
pictures by PAT SCHORIES

HARPER

An Imprint of HarperCollinsPublishers

Woof, woof!

What do you see, Biscuit?

Is it a bird?

Woof, woof!

Is it a butterfly?
Woof, woof!

Oh, Biscuit.

It is a teddy bear!

Woof, woof!

Someone lost a teddy bear.

Who can it be?

Woof, woof!

Woof, woof!

Is this your teddy bear, Sam?

Ruff!

No. It is not Sam's bear.

Woof, woof!

Is this your teddy bear, Puddles?

Bow wow!

No. It is not Puddles's bear.

Woof, woof!

Someone lost a teddy bear.

But who can it be?

Woof, woof!

Wait, Biscuit.

What do you see now?

Woof!

Biscuit sees a big truck.

18

Woof!

Biscuit sees a lot of boxes.

Woof, woof!

Biscuit sees a little boy, too.

Woof, woof! Woof, woof!
Is this your teddy bear,
little boy?

Yes. It is!

Woof!

The little boy
lost his teddy bear, Biscuit,
but you found it!
Woof, woof!

The teddy bear gets a big hug.

Woof, woof!

And Biscuit gets a big hug, too!
Woof!

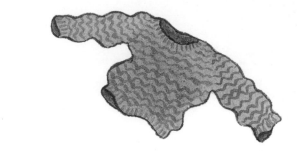